Highland history and cult
www.ambaile.org.uk

For Izzy and Jacob,
my inspiration, who brought
the magic into my world.

Philippa

This book
belongs to

....

First published in 2017 by Firefly Press
25 Gabalfa Road, Llandaff North, Cardiff, CF14 2JJ
www.fireflypress.co.uk
in association with Fairydoorz
PO BOX 250, Penarth, CF64 9FS
www.fairydoorz.co.uk
info@fairydoorz.co.uk

Text © Laura Sheldon; illustrations © Erica Jane Waters
The author and illustrator assert their moral right to be identified as author and illustrator
in accordance with the Copyright, Designs and Patent Act 1988.

A CIP catalogue record of this book is available from the British Library.

ISBN 978-1-910080-53-5

This book has been published with the support of the Welsh Books Council.

Design by Claire Brisley
Printed and bound by Zenith Media, Wales

ADVENTURES THROUGH THE FAIRY DOOR

Sophie Finds a Fairy Door

LAURA SHELDON

ILLUSTRATED BY
ERICA JANE WATERS

Fairydoorz®
Let the magic into your home

As Sophie moved her teddies
From their pile upon the floor,
She gaped and gasped, for she'd revealed
A tiny fairy door!

She lay flat on her tummy
And tap-tapped on the wood.
Then waited by the fairy door,
As quietly as she could.

And sure enough she heard a sound,
A tinkling little bell,
And a softly silver whisper,
Like the ocean in a shell.

The door began to open
And a gentle glow came out.
A sprinkling of fairy dust
Blew in and danced about.

And then out from behind the doo
Appeared a tiny sprit
The silver wings upon her bac
Shimmered in the ligh

'A fairy!' whispered Sophie.
'Is this real or just pretend?'
'I'm Bella,' said the tiny girl,
'Your special fairy friend.'

'You must have been so very good
To find me hiding here,
For only those with hearts of gold
Make fairy friends appear.

'Hold my hand and come with me,
      And through the door we'll go.'

'I'm far too big to fit in there!'
Said Sophie, 'don't you know?'

But Bella waved her silver wand
And gave a little wink.
She sprinkled on some fairy dust
And the girl began to shrink!

Within a moment Sophie was
A fairy height and size.
She gazed around with wonder, and
Could not believe her eyes!

Then through the door the fairy flew
As Sophie held her hand.
She gasped with joy at what she saw:
A glittering fairy land.

A castle grew upon a knoll
And stretched up to a sky
Of shimmering pink and clearest blue,
With fairies fluttering by.

A river flowed towards the sea,
The air was warm and still,
And flowers lined a golden path
That climbed a grassy hill.

'Come on, Sophie,' Bella called,
'Let's fly and look around.'
'Wait for me, I cannot fly!'
Cried Sophie from the ground.

But Bella laughed and spread her arms.
'Believe in magic things!'
And Sophie, to her great surprise,
Had grown some fairy wings!

The pair held hands and spread their wings;
They flew above the trees.
They swooped down to the flowers
With the butterflies and bees.

Then Bella tugged on Sophie's arm
And pulled her up again.
'If we're quick, we've just got time
To catch the tea-cup train!'

They fluttered faster than before,
And soon they came to land
In a teeny-tiny tea-cup,
On a bed of golden sand.

'All aboard the tea-cup train!'
A cheery fairy cried.
The line of tea-cups whizzed along
With Sophie safe inside.

They'd just climbed up the grassy hill
And nearly reached the top.
When suddenly the tea-cup train
Shuddered to a stop!

The fairy at the front called out,
'The tea-cup train won't go!'
'What's wrong?' asked Sophie, climbing out,
But no one seemed to know.

When Sophie reached the first tea-cup
She found a little book.

'The Workings of the Tea-Cup Train,'
She said, 'I'll take a look.'

She read and read, then smiled and said,
'No need to cry and shout.
The tea-cup train's just fine, although
It seems the fuel's run out!'

The Workings
of the
Tea-cup
Train

'What does it run on?' Bella asked.
'What fuels the tea-cup train?'
So Sophie turned back to the book,
And searched it once again.

'Ah-ha!' cried Sophie, jumping up.
'The answer's here, it seems.
The tea-cup train will only run
On fairy dust and dreams.'

Every fairy laughed and said,
'I've fairy dust galore!'
They sprinkled dust upon the train,
And then they sprinkled more.

'Why won't it go?' one fairy moaned,
'We've sprinkled all we've got.'
Then Bella looked at Sophie. 'Well,
There's one thing we forgot.

'The dreams that come from boys and girls
Are powerful and strong.
It's to their imaginations that
The fairy world belongs.

'Would you help us, Sophie?
The magic lies in you.
Dream the tea-cup train can go
And make your wish come true.'

So Sophie squeezed her eyes tight shut,
And wished and wished again.
She pictured all her fairy friends
Upon the tea-cup train.

In her imagination,
Sophie saw the tea-cups go,
'You've done it!' shouted Bella
As the train began to glow.

'All aboard the tea-cup train,'
The cheery fairy cried.
The fairies whooped and rang their bells
And swiftly climbed inside.

'Three cheers for Sophie,'
Bella called. The fairies cried, 'Hooray!'
'She wished and willed and just believed,
And saved our fairy day.'

The train stopped at the fairy door,
And Sophie had to go.
She felt her wings begin to shrink,
Her skin began to glow.

'I think the magic's wearing off,
I better had be going.'
She stepped back through the fairy door,
And felt her body growing.

In no time she was normal-sized,
And crouched down on the floor.
'I've had a truly lovely time
Through the fairy door.'

'I'll see you soon,' said Bella,
And she waved and blew some kisses.
'Remember – keep the fairy land
Alive with dreams and wishes.'

And Sophie moved her teddies,   To keep her sweetest secret safe:
To a pile upon the floor,   The magic fairy door.

FAIRY FINDING GAME

Find and count the fairy items on each
page throughout the story!

Find the...

Fairies

Butterflies

Fairy Doors